Ted Prior

Grug

For Dougal, Lucy and Eve

GRUG GOES TO SCHOOL

Published in Australia and New Zealand in 2009 by Simon & Schuster (Australia) Pty Limited
Suite 19a, Level 1, Building C, 450 Miller Street Cammeray NSW 2062

A CBS Company
Sydney · New York · London · Toronto

Visit our website at www.simonandschuster.com.au

National Library of Australia Cataloguing-in-Publication entry

Author:	Prior, Ted.
Title:	Grug goes to school / Ted Prior.
ISBN:	9780731813933 (pbk.)
Series:	Prior, Ted. Grug.
Target Audience:	For children.
Dewey Number:	A823.3

Cover and internal design: Xou Creative
Printed in China: Phoenix Offset

The paper used to produce this book is a natural, recyclable product made from wood grown in sustainable plantation forests. The manufacturing processes conform to the environmental regulations in the country of origin.

9 8 7 6 5

Ted Prior

Grug

goes to school

SIMON & SCHUSTER
AUSTRALIA
A CBS COMPANY

There was a small school
near Grug's home.

Early one morning Grug went
to take a closer look.

He peered through an open doorway.
No one was inside.

He tip-toed down the hall —
past some schoolbags.

The big chair at the front of the classroom was too high for Grug.

But one of the little chairs was just the right size.

He counted five pencils in a pencil case.

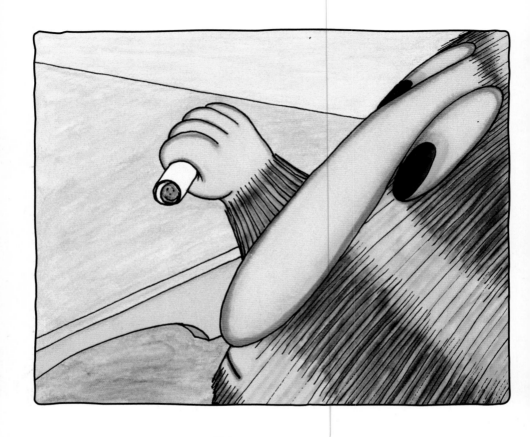

On the big desk he found a stamp.

It made a picture on Grug's hand.

Grug wrote on the blackboard.

Then he found some books to read.

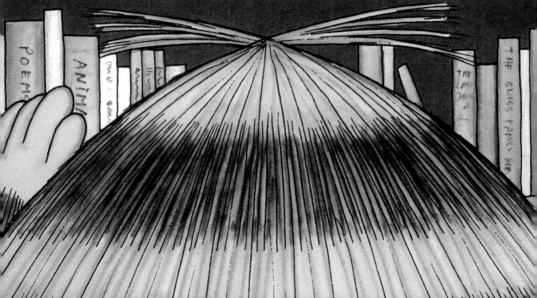

One of them was very exciting!

Suddenly a bell rang and Grug knew
it was time for him to go.

He hurried away towards home ...

… to finish his homework.

Grug

Grug at the beach

Grug and his bicycle

Grug and the big red apple

Grug builds a boat

Grug builds a car

Grug and his garden

Grug goes fishing

Grug goes to school

Grug and the green paint

Grug has a birthday

Grug and his kite

Grug learns to cook

Grug learns to dance

Grug learns to swim

Grug meets Snoot

Grug and his music

Grug in the playground

Grug plays cricket

Grug plays soccer

Grug and the rainbow

Grug goes shopping

Grug at the snow

Grug at the zoo